P9-DWI-407

Dear Parent:
Your child's love of reading starts here!

Every child learns to read in a different way and at his or her own speed. Some go back and forth between reading levels and read favorite books again and again. Others read through each level in order. You can help your young reader improve and become more confident by encouraging his or her own interests and abilities. From books your child reads with you to the first books he or she reads alone, there are I Can Read Books for every stage of reading:

SHARED READING
Basic language, word repetition, and whimsical illustrations, ideal for sharing with your emergent reader

BEGINNING READING
Short sentences, familiar words, and simple concepts for children eager to read on their own

READING WITH HELP
Engaging stories, longer sentences, and language play for developing readers

READING ALONE
Complex plots, challenging vocabulary, and high-interest topics for the independent reader

ADVANCED READING
Short paragraphs, chapters, and exciting themes for the perfect bridge to chapter books

I Can Read Books have introduced children to the joy of reading since 1957. Featuring award-winning authors and illustrators and a fabulous cast of beloved characters, I Can Read Books set the standard for beginning readers.

A lifetime of discovery begins with the magical words **"I Can Read!"**

Visit www.icanread.com for information on enriching your child's reading experience.

I Can Read!™ My First SHARED READING

JUST A KITE

BY MERCER MAYER

HARPER
An Imprint of HarperCollins*Publishers*

For Kyla,
May your kites fly high
and brighten the sky!

www.icanread.com

Library of Congress catalog card number: 2013947668
ISBN 978-0-06-207197-2 (trade bdg.) — ISBN 978-0-06-147814-7 (pbk.)

15 16 17 SCP 10 9 8 7 6 5 4 3 2 ❖ First Edition

A Big Tuna Trading Company, LLC/J. R. Sansevere Book
www.littlecritter.com

I see a kite at the hobby store.

I say, “That’s the one I want.”

We take my new kite home.

I put it together. Dad helps.

Saturday is the Critterville
Kite Flying Contest.
I take my kite out to practice.

My dad and I go to the park.
It is a very windy day.

Dad says, “Watch out for trees!”

Oops, too late.

My kite gets caught.

Dad saves my kite.

But my kite is all ripped up.

I cry.

Dad says, “Don’t worry.

We can get another one.”

But the store is sold out.
I say, "I will miss the contest!"
I am brave and only cry a little.

Dad says, “I have an idea.”

He calls Grandpa.

Grandpa will build a new kite.

Grandpa goes to his workshop.
He builds a special kite
just for me.

Grandpa brings it to me.

It has no decorations on it.
I do some special art on it.
We are ready to try it out.

My kite flies well at the park.
It goes fast. It goes high.
Too high. It disappears.

“Oh, no!” I say. “My kite is gone!”

"Yep, it's gone," says Grandpa.
"The string broke."

“Let’s go shopping.”
I ask, “Why, Grandpa?”
“It’s a surprise,” Grandpa says.

We go to the hardware store.

We go to the lumber yard.

We go to the art supply store.

I ask, “What’s all this stuff for?”

“You’ll see,” says Grandpa.

Grandpa goes to Dad’s shop.

He is there for a long time.
He won't tell me anything
at dinner or at bedtime.

In the morning, I find
Grandpa's surprise for me.
It's an amazing new kite.

HERE
IS THE
JUDGE

We all go to the
Kite Flying Contest.
My kite flies great!

I don’t win a ribbon
for the highest kite
or the fastest kite.

I win a ribbon for the
most original kite!

I say, “It’s just a kite
my Grandpa made for me!”